## About the Author

Jim Teeters is a retired social worker. He received his BA in Sociology from the University of Washington in 1962 and a MSW from the University of Hawaii in 1965. Jim has written and published poetry as well as published books on teaching methods. Currently, he volunteers for his local school district, teaches classes in a women's homeless shelter, and conducts poetry sessions for seniors. He and his wife Rebecca (now deceased) have traveled to over thirty countries and five continents. Jim offers these stories to awaken one's thoughts and feelings about wonder, danger, and shame.

# Short Stories of Wonder, Danger and Shame

Jim Teeters

Short Stories of Wonder, Danger and Shame

Olympia Publishers
*London*

www.olympiapublishers.com
OLYMPIA PAPERBACK EDITION

Copyright © Jim Teeters 2025

The right of Jim Teeters to be identified as author of
this work has been asserted in accordance with sections 77 and 78 of
the Copyright, Designs and Patents Act 1988.

All Rights Reserved

No reproduction, copy or transmission of this publication
may be made without written permission.
No paragraph of this publication may be reproduced,
copied or transmitted save with the written permission of the publisher,
or in accordance with the provisions
of the Copyright Act 1956 (as amended).

Any person who commits any unauthorised act in relation to
this publication may be liable to criminal
prosecution and civil claims for damage.

A CIP catalogue record for this title is
available from the British Library.

ISBN: 978-1-83543-165-8

This is a work of fiction.
Names, characters, places and incidents originate from the writer's
imagination. Any resemblance to actual persons, living or dead, is
purely coincidental.

First Published in 2025

Olympia Publishers
Tallis House
2 Tallis Street
London
EC4Y 0AB

Printed in Great Britain

# Dedication

I dedicate this book to Lorraine Torres, owner of the Harp Bar and Restaurant where I wrote these stories, and to my now-deceased friend Rich Frishholz who I shared drinks and stories at the Harp.

# Acknowledgments

I want to offer my thanks to Rich and Lorraine for their wonderful caring and comfort-giving friendship. I also want to thank longtime friend, Pam Bigelow and my good walking and poetic friend, Nancy Colson for their editing skills.

# Contents

| | |
|---|---|
| Introduction | 13 |
| WONDER | 15 |
| Cave | 18 |
| Who Are You? | 21 |
| Calling | 25 |
| Gift | 27 |
| Yippy | 30 |
| DANGER | 33 |
| Wiener | 36 |
| Witness | 38 |
| Parachute: Life, death; hope, demise | 41 |
| Alone in the Woods | 45 |
| Court Case | 48 |
| SHAME | 51 |
| My, How Time Flies! | 54 |
| Rules | 56 |
| School Library | 58 |
| Null | 62 |
| Reward | 65 |
| TINY TRUE TALES | 67 |
| Ten True Tales of Minor Danger | 74 |
| Ten True Tales of Minor Shame | 79 |

# Introduction

I have used the metaphors of wonder and danger in much of my spiritual thoughts and writing. When these stories popped into my mind and after completing them, they seemed to fit into wonder and danger, but then some offered a look at our human shame. Ironically, the stories (basically fictional but some based on real events) could be evenly divided, six in each category for a total of eighteen short stories.

Here are some brief definitions of each category: Wonder involves surprising, unexpected positive happenings and can include healing, finding lost objects, or finding true love. Danger involves harmful, unpleasant, or injurious happenings and can include pain, illness, death, or losses of any kind. Shame involves foolishness, wrongdoing, or humiliating behaviors and can include harming or hurting someone or something, or anything considered naughty. Our lives are filled with these happenings along with common day-to-day and routine occurrences.

The section titled Tiny True Tales comes from my life and they are evenly divided into ten tiny stories in each category — so a total of thirty tiny true tales. I wrote these to give you, dear reader, an opportunity to think about your own life tales of wonder, danger, and shame.

# WONDER

## SHE! A Plan, the Dream

Karen was three desks ahead of Michael in the Sociology class at the university. "*She is delightful to look at*," he thought, "*but she is also so academic; and me, not so, might make it hard to connect with her.*" The subject of study was important to him, however, he was more of an extrovert social being; and who "*SHE*" was became his main interest in this particular class session.

Karen was so lovely to him, so slender and with long dark hair, often in braids or a pony tail. Her skin was lovely and smooth when she was short sleeved. Her dark eyes seldom looked at him — but when he was presenting and he saw her face, he felt like melting butter before her. Yes, he wished he could be her boyfriend and embrace all her beauty. But she was so serious, focused, and smart, didn't seem possible. When he imagined her in his arms, slender and soft, he readily got aroused and had to move on — but *SHE* was his obsession.

Finally, a few weeks into the session, he boldly decided he wanted to make an attempt to have a romantic connection — but how? He decided to ask his tennis partner, Frank. Frank seemed like such a wise sort and so Michael thought he would be the best choice for his love-coach (he called him). Frank laughed at the idea but agreed to chat about it. Frank had also seen Karen occasionally and agreed that she would be a great girl to love, but he too saw her as a serious, dedicated student — probably no love object.

Michael suggested Frank just listen to his thoughts and ideas and then perhaps they could team up with some kind of direction for him to take. So the dialogue began; Michael described his desires and passion for Karen and then put the question before the two of them — the coach and the player. The plan was that he should boldly go up to her after class and tell her he was attracted to her and wanted to perhaps just go have a coffee and share their stories. "*Share their stories*" — they both thought that was a great opening.

The next session ended and Michael approached her, "Hi Karen, I have wanted to meet you — I've noticed you in class and perhaps we could have a coffee together and share our stories."

"Oh, well I am pretty busy and not quite in the mood for that," *She* responded coldly. "My interest right now is sociology studies, not romance." Michael looked shocked — she even used the term, romance! "I...er...I...he stuttered...ah, okay...sorry." She looked at him with those eyes, but they were more of disgust than any interest. She turned and walked away, textbooks tight in her arms. He reported the encounter to Frank, who said he was sorry but wasn't surprised. "I don't think this is going to work," he said. Michael thought so too, and he ached inside— no *SHE*!

The next week, the professor had decided to form random pairs of students to explore how teamwork can enhance learning and research. Each team of two could select a topic to discuss and research, then write a report to describe their discovery about two things, the topic and the team relationship experience. To Michael's great surprise — *SHE* was to be his partner in this project. When the two were named as partners, she looked again at him with what he interpreted as disgust.

Actually, when they met for coffee, she didn't seem disturbed at all; she even smiled at him and seemed eager to work together. As they discussed their topic, Urban Life and Human Need, they both poured out information they'd studied and their team connection was making progress. In fact, her eyes seemed to show interest in him, as a person, not just an academic.

One evening in her apartment, as they began to tackle the idea of the relationship experience, she even took his hand and thanked him for the time together. They had worked hard and he had just kept his romantic attraction inside, just enjoying the experience. Then she actually bent forward, her lovely face drawing near, and to his utter surprise, *SHE* kissed him on his lips. He almost fainted with pleasure and then tight hugging and more kissing. "I do like being with you," she said. "I do too, so much, Karen."

In the final write-up session in Michael's place after finishing the report, some more kissing. But then another surprise: Karen wrapped her arms around him and then said, "Michael, I love you and I want to make love with you!" It was then that Michael collected his erotically aroused self and said: "I want to make love to you, too, but I want it to be in our consecrated marriage."

*SHE* looked at him and said, "This very moment shows me who you really are and I am so proud of you for that. I want to share my life with you. My trusted love in you and marriage sounds perfect!"

The commitment was made and married they were – Michael and *SHE*! Their first night of love-making brought forth the Dream!

# Cave

Hogan was a recent master's graduate in psychology and now was teaching psychology at the local community college. He was in his late 20s. He loved his job and his students loved him as well. He was creative, fun, and knowledgeable. Now settled down in an apartment, making good money and with vacations throughout the year, he couldn't be happier. He wasn't in a love relationship currently and so he spent his off hours with some guy friends at the local bars, golfing or bowling. He did have a kind of longing, however— not shared with anyone he knew. He wanted to go cave exploring. There was the Orgram Caves not far away that he'd read about. They were part of the state parks offering and seemed mysterious and attractive as an exploration.

    He decided to try that adventure during the spring break. So he got more online information about the caves and how to keep safe in the exploration. There was a shop near the caves, Cave Dweller Shop he heard about that offered some items to help folks explore. There were guided tours in the summer only, but they offered the opportunity to go on your own and suggested beginning with the information and equipment for safe, self-guided tours from the Cave Dweller. So on the first Monday of the spring break, he headed off on his adventure.

    The shop offered nutritious snacks, cave-designed backpacks, and special flashlights that offered several settings for every possible encounter in the dark. Also, he decided as suggested by online guides, to get the bag of "sticker ribbons" which you placed along your way so you can find your way back, the true challenge for cave exploration. Cell phones don't work in there and when you head in you are basically isolated from anything outside.

It was mid-morning when he had gotten some exploration information and the suggested items and faced the cave opening. He knew there were three possible cave channels and decided on the central one, it was the longest and offered challenges he wanted to take on. Part of the information gave him warnings and how to handle the "cave dwellers" which included spiders, snakes, bats, scorpions, etc. According to the information, no bears, wolves, or dangerous cats, hung out in there thankfully.

Sure enough, as he went deeper these creatures appeared — the scariest ones for him were the larger spiders that hung down in webs. Being face-to-face with a spider freaked him out pretty much. A few snakes slithered but they didn't seem dangerous. He was running out of the sticker ribbons, however, so he decided it was time to head back.

Then he heard a noise a kind of moaning sound. Another cave dweller he hadn't learned about? It was a creepy sound and he thought about skipping this but decided to check it out. Then, closer it sounded like someone weeping, a person? He called out, "Hello?" And then he heard a woman's voice, "Help me, I'm hurt!" He climbed over to an edge and looked down with a flashlight. Sure enough, a lovely young woman in dire condition. "I'm coming down, how can I help?"

He learned that her name was Penny, and she had decided to explore the cave too, but no ribbon. She had fallen and had hurt her leg (broken?) badly and couldn't move. This was, she guessed, her third day in this condition. She'd run out of water and food and expected to die. "Oh, but you've come, and I need to get out." "I will gladly help you, here is some water and I have snacks. Let me see if I can get you out."

He saw her ankle swollen and obviously seemed broken. He grabbed some wrap he'd taken as a caution and it was just what she needed. He fixed it tight. Hogan asserted, "Now we have to get you out of here!" Her face seemed less stressed now that she had water and snacks. But she was stuck. "Oh Hogan, what can you do?" she sobbed "Let me think." He pondered and then came up with a quite difficult, but only-way, out plan: "I will shift my backpack to the front and you must wrap your arms around my neck and shoulders and I will carry you out on my back." She was shocked, but it seemed like a plan. "Oh, can you carry me?" "Let's give it a try." He replaced his backpack to the front and let her reach around him from the back. She seemed capable of hanging on. "Ok, let's go," he said.

And, oh the path back, such a struggle, but she hung on and he moved slowly. They'd stop at each ribbon; talk a bit about their lives, snack, and drink water. She was a graduate student on spring break, studying archeology (the cave trip was a kind of learning experience she wanted). The exiting took several hours and they kind of grew close, personally as well as physically. Hogan was getting exhausted but kept going — Penny was barely able to hang on, but kept on, too. Finally, they arrived at the entrance and Hogan was able to call 911 for her rescue. As she was ready to let go she whispered in his ear. "I love you!" Hogan didn't know what to say, just, "Oh, ah," then the sound of sirens.

He came the next day to visit her at the hospital. Her parents were there as well as a brother. They thanked him and hugged him, then said they'd take a break and let him and Penny talk. Hogan looked at Penny and said, "*I Love You*!" They hugged, kissed, and well, from what I heard they got married and both went on archeology finds, but not in caves!

# Who Are You?

Burk Sloan was a sad case. He had been doing well in his youth, finishing high school and then entering a community college and general studies, still wondering about the direction of his life. He was very much in love with Drew Cameron, his love since high school but he was devastated when she decided to stop the relationship. It wasn't because she didn't love Burk but because she wanted to pursue her life goal of completing college and getting into graduate studies for her dream job in human services. She would need to leave the area and want to concentrate on her studies, not loving a guy.

It was soon after she left him that he became severely depressed and quit college. He had left his parents' home, and gladly, because his life with them had not been pleasant. His father was very busy and not caring much about him, his mother had mental health issues that made her cold and distant. They weren't mean people, just incompetent at parenting. They did support him in his college life, but soon after he quit. What happened is that he became an alcoholic, homeless, and hopeless (he would readily agree). He was despondent and used what money he got from his parents for drinking and occasionally finding a cheap motel to survive the cold and rain.

One dark night, he was weakly walking in the alley near his motel and favorite bar, and he kind of stumbled into a sort of cavern. There was a wooden box where he sat to swig from his whiskey decanter. Then a voice:

"Welcome to my cavern, Burk, been waiting for you."

"What the hell!" Burk croaked. He saw no one as he looked around.

"Truly, I care about you and what has happened to you," the voice continued.

Burk thought of running, but he was too drunk for that and the voice was in some way soothing. He drunkenly decided to continue this weird moment. "Who are you, and why can't I see you?"

"I am the Cavern Counselor, sent from spiritual forces to rescue you from your dismal life, wanna continue?"

"Go on...," Burk muttered.

"I am going to ask you some questions and then you can ponder each and return with your answers, just at night, and only you."

"Go on..."

"Each question is to help you move forward in your life, and I believe you will, regardless of how doubtful you may feel."

"Go on..."

"The first question is, "Who are you? Go away now and ponder that and come and tell me tomorrow night. Farewell son."

"Son, what?" Burk somehow decided to leave and do just that. Somehow he felt a kind of assurance about this strange encounter, but he was so despondent he thought, "Why not?"

The next night, he sat in the cavern, but without the decanter and he was sober. "Are you here, Cavern Counselor?"

"Yes, and your answer?"

Burk had thought about it all day and he came up with this. "I am someone who has fallen in my life. I am injured and hurt, but in finding you, I feel like I want to heal. Part of who I am is empathetic and caring. In my school life, I was often the kid who listened and helped others. I think that's who I really am not this selfish, alcoholic self-centered person. Deep inside I am caring. It's got to come out again, but, how?"

"You are on your way, so the next question is, what do you want to be? See you tomorrow."

The next night, Burk answered, "I want to find a way to climb free of this despair and find a way to help the people who are just like me, homeless and hopeless."

Cavern Counselor, "What do you want to do? See you tomorrow."

Burk sobered up for this next night's encounter and came up with a dream plan. He entered the cavern. "I want to create a way to offer housing and develop a program for people like me."

"What steps do you need to take, Burk? See you next time."

The next night, Burk had a plan. "I want to quit drinking, now. I want to return to college to prepare for the designing of a program and find a way to finance it."

"When you finish your plan, come and see me."

Here is what happened: Burk did quit drinking (well, he did sip a wine now and then). He convinced his parents to help him with some finances but he also got a simple coffee shop job to sustain himself. At his graduation time, he wrote a paper about a program he called Discovery Center. His paper provided a plan, which impressed his professor so much that the professor contacted a rich guy he knew, who was trying to find a way to use his wealth for a good purpose. That began the first Discovery Center. The center provided housing for twenty people, a program that took them through a process similar to the Cavern Counselor questions. Each person had a plan and it worked – all twenty found a way forward and then a new twenty members were found. Soon, more grants were offered to expand the program to other locations.

Burk decided it was time to return to the cavern. So one night he went down the alley and into the cavern, but no Counselor. He came out, and someone was approaching him. It was Drew!

Drew reached for him, "I want you back in my life, you marvelous, guy! In fact, I want to join your Discovery Center program to offer my human services!"

Burk blurted out: "Hired! And how about let's get married and form a team!"

"Perfectly put," Drew said hugging him, so the team was formed!

# Calling

Ken Roberts is a hippie sort. We're back in the 70s when such guys were prevalent. Most were just atheists, scrambled away from their church past. Ken is a professional social service guy, traveling and training in his profession. He is a church member, not too impressed with the seeming self-righteous ones. But he likes to volunteer to help and the church is a quiet kind of place, not a lot of hoopla.

Ken is married with kids and though he is gone a lot in his travels, he is a good husband and dad. But on the road, he is a partier, drinking and smoking dope with others of the same ilk. He quiets down when home, but still has his wine-time. His wife is a good woman, a good mother, and is appreciated by the church folks. Ken, however, is known as one who doesn't quite fit the ideal church member mode.

However, he was selected as one of the committee members for the job of selecting the needed person for the Associate Pastor position. The last Associate had gone on to another job, so they needed to find a replacement. The job description was shared with the committee, mainly working on religious education, kid, and youth programs. This person also filled in for the head pastor, Reverend John Harding's sermons, etc., when he was gone; so a good responsible, and trustworthy Christian person. After a few meetings, there seemed to be no applicants available or eligible. The next meeting was set and it ended in a forceful prayer by Reverend John.

Ken headed off on one of his working trips. He loved this particular town. It was on the coast, nice motel and great bars nearby for partying. After a day of work, he decided to go on a pre-partying walk on the beach, where there were caves and high rocks – such beauty. One cave was really a tunnel from the beach out to the ocean waves. He decided to walk the tunnel and as he approached the ocean view he heard a voice, "You will be the Associate Pastor, Ken!" This voice was like an echo but it came from nowhere. Ken thought a bit then said, "Is that you, God?" The answer was clear, "*Yes*!" Then Ken yelled out… "Noooo! not me!" Answer, "Yes, *You*!"

Ken was rightly stunned. First, because of the voice, and second, because he was the least likely person to be chosen for that position, given his lifestyle. So, given what he experienced, he thought, "Ha, no one would ever suggest me for that position." And he spoke to the voice, seemingly now gone, "If anyone suggests me, then OK, but they won't!" He kind of chuckled, realizing how safe he was, but had made the pledge: "If anyone!" He felt safe and comfortable; then off to his partying.

Back to the meeting, the chairman asked if there were any new possibilities. Reverend John looked at Ken, "Ken, I have been praying and considering this and God tells me that you are to be my Associate Pastor!" (Inside Ken's head was a cry "Noooo…!" — but he had made the promise…"if anyone!" He responded, "John I am shocked, but I will be willing to do what you and God wish." The committee members smiled and agreed to accept Ken into the position. And, so it was.*

*This is based on a true story.*

# Gift

Sue Ellen was born in a stable, middle-class home in a small college town. Her dad worked in the local supermarket and her mom stayed at home and watched her and her younger brother, Billie. Sue Ellen and Billie played happily together during their young lives. One of their play spaces was the guest room with a rickety single bed — they jumped on it and laughed. Their mom had warned them about being careful not to jump too hard since the bed was not in so good shape.

One afternoon Sue Ellen and Billie were doing their jumping fun on the bed (She was at age five and him at three). Billie got off and hid under the bed while Sue Ellen kept jumping, then down went the bed right on top of Billie. He wasn't hurt and kept laughing, but he was trapped. For some reason, Sue Ellen didn't go running for their mom; she told Billie, "Lie still." He did. She reached down with one hand, slipped two fingers under the railing, and lifted the bed off Billie. She was stunned but felt she would not tell and asked Billie not to say anything about her lifting the bed. When their dad got home she watched as he struggled to lift the bed up and prop it so he could fix the leg. Even at five years she realized something was happening, but knew she shouldn't tell. Billie didn't even mention getting trapped and she was glad for that.

Now an adolescent, Sue Ellen was going on her usual walk in the woods, something she found soothing and it was helping her be fit, too. As she rounded a turn in the path a large tree had fallen and blocked the way. She, again simply reached under the trunk and threw the tree off the path — then she heard a voice: "You have a gift that must only be used in times of need, as this. Never use this gift for your own delight. You'll be a blessing if you do as you've heard. Keep your gift as your secret, too."

"Who are you?" she pleaded. No answer. But she knew in her heart it was the source of her strength and she was willing to follow the command. Somehow she felt comfortable and cared for by this unseen source.

Over several years and into college she had moments where she used this gift. One was at her job in the same supermarket as her dad. He was off and a troubled guy pulled on a display shelf. Just before it collapsed on him, she stopped the fall and quickly moved away. The guy was flabbergasted at the saving and wandered off confused but glad. Another time she was driving at night and saw a car careen into a ditch. She jumped out and pulled the car free, running back to her car and disappearing. In a summer swim time, she saw a girl struggle and go underwater — possibly drowning. She dived down, pushed the girl to the lake edge, and quickly swam underwater not to be seen.

An incident that became a time changer was when the old sports bleachers at her college collapsed and she pushed them back. Some saw her do this, but her face was unseen, so the story hit the local newspaper: *Super Girl Saves Dozens (But who is she?)*

Paul Barker, a college student, read the story and became obsessed with finding out who she was. He began watching girls on campus and kind of using his intuitive skills to locate the one. He somehow was led to Sue Ellen, sitting in the school cafeteria, and sidled up with his meal. He introduced himself and asked her what she was studying. "I'm an education major now, what about you, Paul?"

"I'm working on computer science." Then Paul asks, "Did you see the article about the "super girl?"

She hesitated and he knew this was her. "Ah...yeah, crazy huh?"

They finished their meals, and he asked if she'd like to have coffee sometime. She liked Paul's looks and manner and answered, "Yeah, sure." And they exchanged phone numbers.

Then one night a car spun out of control near the college. The passenger, a young woman, was thrown under the car — trapped and yelling for help. Sue Ellen was coming out of her college meeting session and ran forward, grabbing the back of the car. As she lifted the car the front was raised too and the young woman scrambled out. The driver was obviously drunk and now unconscious. As Sue Ellen dropped the car the front went down too. Paul was at the front end. "It was you, Sue Ellen – Super Girl!" Paul yelled.

"Yikes, and what about you, Paul?"

Paul answered, "I think we both have had the same gift and that visitation!"

The young girl had run off, and Paul called nine-one-one to deal with the driver. "Sue Ellen, can we go have some supper?"

Sue Ellen smiled, "OK."

Over dinner, they each shared similar stories and the voices they both heard. After sharing they took a walk around campus and Paul said, "I think we belong together." Sue Ellen was kind of surprised but somehow felt the same way.

Sue Ellen and Paul became lovers and eventually wed. On the wedding night, they both heard the voice: "Now you've met and married, and you will no longer have the gift, but you will have a child, and that child will receive the gift."

# Yippy

A program was started for students needing help, by Superintendent Bob Garfield, called the Youth Progress Program or YPP — which easily got called Yippy. The plan is to encourage students and parents to enroll in this program if the student is having academic issues. The program is designed to be just three months and then kids return to regular school programs and the hope is they'll function normally. The program operates two times in the first part of the year — giving the opportunity for kids to return to regular educational programming. The staff meets in the late summer and plans the program — kids from last year then enter the YPP in the fall, and kids from the fall quarter enter the YPP in the winter session. The staff of YPP includes the director, three teachers, and one educational assistant. The program includes sixty failing students — so each teacher has twenty students working to help the kids improve.

Unfortunately, the program itself had been failing over the last three years and Bob had decided to give it one more year before closing it down. The staff, who had offered so much energy, were despondent and fearful for the program and their jobs. What to do? The staff consisted of the director, Donna, three teachers, Bill, Barbara, and Karen, as well as an educational assistant, Connie. Each of them was hard working, but the program was pretty much based on the normal educational aspects, just like the school they served; so no particular progress was made.

During the summer preparation meeting, Donna came with a great big smile on her face; unusual for her. And lately, she had scowled even more. The team was surprised and asked her what was going on. "I had an amazing dream last night; in fact, it was a visitation, I think."

"Well, tell us!" Connie said.

"Ok, I will, I had been so down about our possible demise and went to bed with tears in my eyes. Then the dream: A woman dressed in a graduation outfit stood before me as I was seated in our meeting room. She said her name was 'Learning Laura' and she would offer us a plan to succeed. She laid out the plan saying, there are four forces for best learning, and she named them:

One: Students need to feel safe, they must be a part of the planning program, and they must be considered and treated like special people: listened to, respected, and trusted.

Two: Students need to be stimulated by exciting program aspects, lots of action, exploration, and discovery, and rewarded for their progress. The students should also be teachers of each other.

Three: The program must be systematic, where it is clear what the goals are. Students being a part of this planning process should be able to understand in each lesson what is expected of them and what will be the aim.

Four: The learning must also be spontaneous and surprising, with lots of fun and laughter.

She added "Our program will be a success if we follow those guidelines and involve students in teamwork. May you, your team, and your students find great success this year!" Then Learning Laura came over to me and placed her hands on my shoulders and said a prayer I couldn't quite hear, but I felt so blessed and positive — that is why I'm smiling!"

The team was stunned by what they heard, but "Let's get started!" Connie yelled.

That next session was a complete change. Instead of 'students,' they were referred to as Learning Team Members (LTM's). The LTM's joined with the teachers in planning using the four forces. The staff listened and supported them and together they created a safe, stimulating, systematic, and spontaneous endeavor.

Results: When the students returned to the regular classrooms, they all made great progress and grades, even winning prizes for academic achievement. And these students even offered help to the teachers in planning and improving the teaching methods!

The program was extended and expanded and other school districts created their — YPPYs! Yippie!

# DANGER

## The Saga of the Lost Foot: Desperation and Desire

I work together with Tom in a machine shop with lots of cutting tools. We named one "the slicer" because we can cut logs, boards, and even metal rods and pipes in just moments. One evening after everyone had left, even the supervisor, we were completing a job due in the morning. What happened created a mystery for both of us.

As we were slicing logs, Tom slipped on an oily spot on the floor and the slicer cut off his left foot just above the ankle. It sliced cleanly his tibia and fibula bones. He immediately fell down. I grabbed a strap and rag to cover the end and stopped the bleeding. I also grabbed the foot and quickly bagged it in a plastic container, then called 911 to report it. I wanted him to be safe while help arrived. He moaned and wailed and I tried to comfort him, but I needed to go out to open the shop doors, which were on the ground level, we were in the basement.

I reached the outer doors and waited for the sirens. It seemed forever, but soon the EMTs and ambulance arrived and they ran in with the first aid equipment and stretcher. I guided them down to the lower level over to where Tom lay, but Tom was not there, nor was the bag with his foot! The team of helpers looked weirdly at me, wondering if was I the one needing mental illness help. There was the blood as evidence, but where was Tom? We all searched and found no trace of his existence. How could he have even moved with only one foot, but he was gone? After an hour of puzzled searching, the team left saying to call again if he appears.

He did appear, just moments after they left. He called me as he stepped out of the storage room, walking normally with both feet! I almost fainted from the startling sight. I gasped and almost screamed – but he headed over and grabbed and hugged me.

"Let me tell you the story," Tom said, "you may not believe it but my foot is the evidence to convince you."

"I'm ready to hear your story," I muttered still shaking. And here is what he told me:

He had lain desperately, groaning and feeling hopeless. Then he heard a voice coming from inside the storage room – a strange voice, like a creature – but it was discernable.

"Come hop into this room and you will find healing – bring your foot." It said. Tom said he thought he had gotten delusional but the voice sounded so confident and convincing that he did just that. He gripped the table, grabbed the footbag, and hopped painfully toward the storage room. He said the door opened and the creature, who had called to him, was a large friendly guy. Well, he said a guy, but he described him as a large hairy being dressed in a golden suit, not one button or zipper.

When he entered the room, he was suddenly somehow carried, or flew into the darkness and then into a large beautiful bedroom. On the bed was a lovely woman in a nightgown, so thin you could see her lovely body. She was dark-haired, slender, and shapely. It was then he said he had the strangest feeling of desperation and desire!

"This is very simple," she said. "I want you to make love to me, and you will find healing for your foot."

For some reason, Tom believed her. "This may be a delusion," he thought, then he muttered, "But what the hell!" And he hopped toward the bed. He dropped his pants, took off his shirt and underwear, and stood naked before her. She removed her nightgown and lay naked with her arms open. He hobbled in and soon was in complete ecstasy, making love to this woman who sighed and laughed, in her ecstasy. This continued until both were completely spent and satisfied. It was then that he noticed his foot back on! Then the darkness again and he felt the presence of the creature guy.

"How did you get out?" I asked.

"The creature told me to run, so I ran into the darkness and then I saw you."

We both went back to work the next week. He was very careful; the other workers or the supervisor never knew what happened.

To be honest, I have since then, often thought of dropping my leg in the slicing machine!

# Wiener

John Porter and his 12-year-old son Jason headed off to go tent camping in the forested mountain area. They packed up food, a tent, sleeping bags, comfort mats, and all needed items. On the way, John told Jason a funny story: "We are headed for bear country and I remember a story a forest ranger told. He said, 'When you head out to the forest where there might be bears you need to have these three things: First, bear bells on your walking stick to warn bears of your presence, second, you need pepper spray in case you are confronted by a bear, and thirdly you need to know what bear scat looks like. Someone in the audience asked me how do you know if it's a bear scat? I answered, you know it's bear scat because it has bear bells and pepper spray cans in it!'" Jason laughed, "Oh, no Dad, hope we don't get a bear attack!"

"Well we do have bear bells for my walking stick but no pepper spray. I don't think we'll have to worry."

"Oh, good…just hiking, cooking, and sleeping; without getting eaten is good, Dad."

"Sounds like a plan!"

Soon they were at the camping area and they set up their tent. It was getting dark and John cooked up some stew he'd brought. "We'll get our hot dogs tomorrow—the best" They laid out the sleeping bags after cooking up yummy S'mores. John dragged in the ice chest and other food items to keep them safe. Then off to bed.

Jason woke up and heard growling outside the tent. "Dad, wake up...I think I hear a bear!" John woke up and listened, "I don't hear anything." Jason said, "Well, I did!" John unzipped the tent door and sure enough a black bear was just outside the tent sniffing at the fire pit. Then the bear looked right at John and moved toward the tent. "Oh, lordy, Jason, what are we going to do?" "Dad, maybe the bear would like the wieners? We could throw some out and see." Jason reached into the ice chest and ripped open the package of wieners. He gave them to John, and he threw one out past the bear. The bear turned and consumed the wieners. Then Jason threw another two out further past the bear and off went the bear in pursuit. John went out of the tent and threw two more further. The bear headed in that direction. Jason came out went closer to the bear and threw out the wieners way further. Soon the bear just gobbled up the wieners and drifted on.

Their sleep was a little lighter but fortunately, there were no more bear noises. "Jason, your wiener plan saved us; let's just go home, and buy some wieners on the way and have our hot dogs at home."

"Good idea Dad!"

# Witness

Rita was a great high school student; with good grades, good friends, activities, and even a girls' soccer team. Now headed to college in Overton several miles through the farm country, she just got a car from her supportive parents, so she was packed and ready to go to Belfield University to study. Her plan was to get her degree in World History, and Belfield was known to have a wonderful history degree, even a graduate degree offering. She was thrilled and ready to go!

The trip would take about 5 or 6 hours and she knew of a couple of rest stops on that route, which made her feel comfortable for the long trip. She had made the trip with her parents a few months ago. She turned on the radio music and hummed her way down the two-lane highway. There were farmlands and a few forest vistas on the way, lovely sights to her today.

She needed to stop for the restroom and she came to the first rest stop and parked under some heavy trees to shade her car from the sun. She did her toileting and as she came out she noticed a car had pulled in and next to the other toilet container she saw a guy with a huge knife raising it and stabbing another guy in the neck. The guy fell bleeding. The murderer spotted Rita and looked surprised, not realizing she was there. She pulled out her phone and dialed 911. But he quickly ran over to her, knocked the phone out of her hand, and grabbed her by the arm. He raised the knife and she quickly kicked him in the crotch, which caused him to drop the knife and collapse in screaming pain. She ran to her car and as she drove to the road she noticed him getting up and heading to his car.

She sped down the road but noticed his car racing to catch up. There were twists and turns in the road and she wasn't all that adept at going so fast on such a curvy path. His car came closer and closer and then the road straightened out along pastures. She stepped up the speed, but he still came closer. Then she noticed a farmer guy standing in a field and a road that turned toward him. She skidded to a near stop and turned in toward the man. She screeched to a halt, got out and the other car came skidding behind her almost hitting her car. She ran toward the guy, kind of young and looking strong.

As she raced towards him she heard the chaser yell, "Watch out, that bitch stole my money, stop her!"

She gasped out, "No, I didn't he's a murderer." The young man muttered, "I believe you; let's pretend I am trapping you." For some reason, she trusted him, "Yes," she said and he grabbed her and whispered, "Stay calm." "Look out she'll kick you in the balls!" the guy screamed as he came racing, holding the knife behind his back. "Got her!" the young man shouted. Then when the guy approached him the young man dropped the girl and headlocked the guy. "Grab some rope," he gasped. She saw the rope next to the fence and together they held and tied the guy up. He had dropped the knife and now was caught. "He murdered a guy back at the rest stop and he saw me look," she said. The guy swore and yelled but then the young guy wrapped a rag around his head and he lay silent and despondent. The young guy introduced himself, "I'm Mike – this is my folk's farmland." "I'm Rita," she replied and they shook hands. Mike used his phone to dial 911 and the operator had heard of the incident from the police, from the found phone. "Where are you?" Mike explained their situation and where they were. Soon there were police sirens blaring, and the police arrived.

They had found the dead guy by following Rita's phone left operating on the ground. They had her phone and soon they took the murderer to the police car handcuffed. The police kept Rita and Mike separated and asked them each about what happened. They wanted two separate stories to check the details and get the facts. After the questioning and getting the contact information from Rita, the investigation and arrest ended. Mike came to Rita and both of them looked lovingly at each other. "You saved my life," Rita said. "You made my day," Mike responded in humor and they each had a craving for a big hug but that didn't seem proper. So, Rita returned to her car and headed to college, arriving quite late. She was able to get her dorm room but skipped dinner, not feeling at all hungry after the trauma of the day.

The following week she started classes. Her favorite class choice was Introduction to World History for the history majors. She arrived at the class and grabbed her desk looking over the handouts and the required textbook. The professor was scribbling on the blackboard in preparation. Then into the room came Mike! She stood up and they both looked shocked. Regardless of the class full of students they walked toward each other and hugged.

# Parachute: Life, death; hope, demise

Mark and Gomer were working late and alone. The rest of the crew from Heavy Tailor Shop had left for the day. The shop was 56th floor of the Cordon Building in Seattle. The shop took the whole top floor of the building and produced canvas and other materials for covers on a variety of items; golf carts, tents, upholstery, etc. Various cutting, stapling, and stitching devices were what the workers used to produce these products. Mark and Gomer had to do finishing work on some items needed the next day for one of their best customers.

Mark was the humorous, extroverted one – plus a kind of let-it-flow fellow. Gomer was the more serious, conservative, money seeker, plus a nose to the grindstone guy. Mark, because of his extroverted skills was also in sales. Gomer was hoping to one day take over the business. Even though they were quite different, they got along just fine as laborers, even sharing lunchtimes and skipping political talk. Both were single, had no love interests, and in their late twenties.

Then that very night it happened. It was midsummer and daylight around 8 p.m., the "Seattle Big One" finally hit, it was an earthquake expected to happen. Well, it did! The Cordon Building had been constructed during the safe-earthquake building period, but it shook and ended up slanted. The electrical went out, the stairs collapsed, and when in panic Mark and Gomer opened the door, there was no way to get down. They did have access to the rooftop. They both climbed up and out to see what had happened. The seventy six -story Columbia Building had disappeared, the famous Space Needle lay down, and they saw folks from the lower level running away. Gomer reached for his cell phone, but it was dead. They were stuck. What could they do?

Mark and Gomer each had different plans so cooperation at this point was not an option. Gomer decided to create a large "help me" sign out of the material at their disposal. His idea was to expect helicopters to begin circling. Mark, on the other hand, decided to create a parachute for a jump, Gomer just laughed at that and got busy. Mark also got busy. There was a gas generator available for some cutting, stapling, and sewing.

Mark had never made a parachute, but he got busy constructing what he imagined from seeing parachutes. He gathered the lightest material and created a large circular shape with lines made out of strips of canvas. Gomer spent his time cutting clear white materials into large letters, they had to be very large!

The morning light broke and Mark had finished his parachute. Gomer was on the roof trying to make the sign stable and visible. Mark climbed to the roof and brought his tool kit strapped to his waist. He had created a kind of loop for a seat his legs straddled and straps for gripping. He looked at Gomer— who didn't even look back as Mark gathered up the large material chute and jumped. "Goodbye!" he yelled. Gomer just laughed and didn't even try to see him.

Mark sailed down very wobbly, twisting and turning uncontrollably. He seemed to be floating down at a good speed but had no control of the lateral moves. He moved too quickly to another building with large windows that were still standing. Somehow his chute got caught on the roof and he swung rapidly into the building face and smashed through a third-story window landing painfully on an apartment floor. He wasn't hurt; just in pain from landing. He looked up to see a beautiful woman in shock looking at him with a toddler in her arms.

"Have you come to save us?" She asked.

"Yes," he said. He was feeling so shaken, but somehow glad to be alive and now facing a challenge, to save them! *"Can I,"* he wondered.

"Well, it was pretty much an accident, but I will help us all get down," he added. She looked pleased.

"How," she asked.

"I'll get started. I think I can lower you down first, then the child, what's his name?"

"Charlie," she said holding him close. "And how do you lower us down?"

"I'm going to create a lowering band. You'll go first and then retrieve Charlie as I lower him."

Mark got to work, using his tool belt; he made a strong strap with a loop for straddling. He pretty much guessed the distance. "OK, let's put you in the loop and I'll lower you. Can Charlie just sit on the couch and feel safe?" he asked.

"Yes, he's smart." She hugged him and told him to sit and the man will get you down to me. "Ah, what's your name?"

"I'm Mark, and you?"

"Patricia."

"Let's start." He wrapped her in the loop, knocked the broken glass away, and helped her out the window where she began to slowly fall with Mark holding tight. Charlie seemed interested and not afraid. Mark watched as Patricia reached the ground, waved, and called, "I'm here." She stepped out of the loop and Mark pulled the strap up. "Your turn, Charlie," he said and wrapped Charlie snugly into the loop. When Charlie saw the distant ground, he began to cry. Mark hugged him and said, "See mommy down there," she wants you to come down." Charlie calmed and Mark lowered him down and safely into the arms of his mom.

Then Mark called down, "Just leave the loop down, and I'll lower me." He tied the strap to the heavy couch and climbed out the window. He had never done this before but he seemed to have the strength necessary for it. He slowly lowered himself using his feet to tighten about the strap. When he reached the ground the beautiful Patricia wrapped her arms around him in complete care and affection!

Here's what happened, the Cordon Building collapsed. Gomer gone! Helicopters were circling too late. Mark, Patricia, and Charlie became a family. She had lost her boyfriend and father of Charlie in an auto accident shortly after Charlie was born. They had planned to marry. But now Mark became her husband and Charlie's stepdad. Mark became involved with the government reconstruction organization that helped rebuild Seattle. No more Columbia Building, but the Space Needle was standing again.

# Alone in the Woods

Claudia opened her eyes. She was sitting on a fallen tree trunk. She was alone and completely devoid of knowing where or why. She felt a sharp pain in the back of her head. Claudia was a nursing student and quickly diagnosed her pain, "a concussion," she surmised. Leaving her to think about "where, how, why, when, who." The "who" started her memories: she knew if she had a concussion, there was a great chance that she had lost memory of what immediately followed the accident...so she pondered back as far as she could remember.

She was on a hiking trip with her friends, Rob, Kellie, Kathy, and Barber. The last thing she remembered was approaching a high cliff. This makes her think, "Yes, I must have fallen." She was always the last one on the hiking trips. She'd be far behind, slow of pace, given the back pain that slowed her down. Her friends would end up at a restaurant, and she'd show up a few minutes later. So, her thoughts were now that she fell, they continued on, and she was uncertain if they knew yet that she was missing.

She realized she was without her phone because it was in her backpack, another memory. She had taken off her backpack as she approached the cliff to get a drink of water from her bottle. She vaguely remembered dropping her bottle, reaching for it, and no more memory. She surmised it was then she fell, hit her head, and perhaps rolled down the cliff. Now sitting on the log, she also surmised she had come partially awake then maybe walked some and then sat. "Just a conjecture," she thought, "but it makes sense."

"OK, here I am, now what?" The feeling of loneliness and panic started to set in. She saw no evidence of the cliff, so she was completely lost and alone in the woods! She had no phone, no water, no sense of what to do. Then she told herself, "You must calm down and face this taking one step at a time, but what is my first step?"

After getting a bit of calm, Claudia decided the first step was to check her own body. If she'd fallen, what else besides the concussion happened? She stood up and checked her body movement. She found only some minor scratches on her arms and calves. Her clothes were pretty much in ok shape, so she felt thankful for not much injury or damage. She felt both thirsty and hungry. This worried her. She noticed some blackberry bushes. She scarfed down some berries and that helped her feel a little better.

Her next step, she decided, was to see if she could follow her path back to where she might have fallen. She scoured the area and found some trampled grasses. "Must be my path," she surmised. She slowly followed what looked like the path but she felt very uncertain. However, she kept trudging, grabbing berries as she went. "I think I'm making my way back," she thought and it seemed so. She now noticed a rising cliff formation. Nothing like what she had last seen from above, so she kept at it. Then she found herself, below a cliff, looking up she felt like, "This is it!" Then she noticed something shiny in the bushes, "Wow, my water bottle!" she blurted out loud. This is where I fell. She saw rocks and guessed the concussion was from that encounter. She must have hit the highest rock before tumbling and she noticed that the grasses were pressed down. The fall on the rock was highest up, then she tumbled more safely to the bottom. She grabbed the bottle and drank quickly, feeling some relief.

Then the sound that shocked her...it sounded like heavy breathing. She looked over and there stood staring at her, a cougar. It was hunched down and looked like it was ready to pounce. She froze, and thought about what was suggested for such an encounter: to stand tall, play dead? Now her whole being shook with fear – "This is it," she thought.

"Claudia!" She heard a yell. It was Rob. He, obviously, saw the cougar and stood a ways away holding a heavy branch and he ran toward the cat screaming and waving the branch – the cougar got the message and turned and ran. "Claudia, what happened?"

"I fell down and hurt my head, a concussion I am sure. Just found my way back – I had wandered unconscious into the woods."

"Oh, we found you!" Behind him appeared the others, Kellie, Kathy, and Barber. There was a wild hugging spree, and the group told Claudia how they had waited too long to find her. "We finally decided to go looking, we found your backpack, and then noticed the cliff markings where you'd fallen."

Claudia and Rob hugged and Rob said, "I've wanted to hug you like this for a long time, Claudia! "Me, too!" Claudia muttered and that began a relationship the others had not predicted. It all happened because a woman found herself alone in the woods!

# Court Case

Carl Handel, a Social Worker, was employed by the state Child Welfare Services (CWS) agency. All kinds of cases came through, mostly families with wayward kids, runaways, and kids in danger. The service was provided as needed not like the Child Protective Services (CPS) agency, where the agency could take control because of illegal or dangerous family behaviors. No, the CWS agency was there for kids and families who needed help and wanted it. If the CWS staff felt a legal option was needed then they'd go to court to take charge.

Well, Carl was on duty when a kid appeared at the office, brought in by police who found him homeless and drug or alcohol addicted. The kid was willing to get help. He was cold, scared, and knew he needed help. This kid was Wilbur, a -13-year-old kid, who Carl discovered was angry at his mom, and his mom was glad to get rid of him. For whatever reason, the two just didn't get along. Wilbur needed some other way to live, not with his angry mom and not on the street. So Carl offered a solution; to begin with, Wilbur could live in a temporary youth facility licensed by the agency. Wilbur was willing but he would miss the drug and alcohol resources that he found on the street.

Another thing Carl learned was that Wilbur attended a middle school and was a pretty good student when he was stable, even at home, and he was appreciated by the school principal, Mrs. Barton. She came to discover Wilbur's dilemma and that CWS was involved in her outreach to Wilbur's mom. Carl discovered that Wilbur also liked Mrs. Barton, for her gentleness and accepting of him. So, Wilbur had some positives going for him.

The next step was to go to court, where Carl wanted to get a legal right to provide a more permanent placement. There Wilbur would not only get shelter but also substance abuse treatment and schooling. Wilbur was willing because he had come to trust Carl. So, the court date was set and Mrs. Barton was invited, as was his mother to be witnesses as necessary. Carl presented his case to the judge.

"Your Honor, given all the details of this case and Wilbur's willingness to be placed in a group home for youth with substance abuse issues, CWS recommends such a placement in Graham Youth Service Center Facility."

"Are there any other comments in this regard?" asked the judge.

"Yes, Your Honor," it was Mrs. Barton. "Your Honor, I am Wilbur's school principal and he is comfortable with me. I would like to suggest that my husband, Tom Barton and I be foster parents for him. I do not believe he has such serious drug use issues; it is only based on the troubling situation at his home. If he is with me, he can continue in his good student work and have a comfortable home."

"So, you and your husband are willing, Mrs. Barton to become licensed foster parents for Wilbur?"

"Yes, Your Honor!"

"I am ordering CWS to license you as foster parents and as soon as that is complete, Wilbur will be under your care."

"Thank you, Your Honor."

"This case is hereby closed and directions will be written and followed by those involved."

Carl was very disappointed and he felt quite certain that his plan would be best, but 'what's done is done,' so the CWS did what was ordered and the Bartons' were licensed as foster parents for Wilbur within two weeks.

Then two weeks after his placement at the Barton's, Carl got a call from Mr. Barton.

"Mr. Handel, I need your help. I came home last night earlier than usual, and my wife and Wilbur were making out, half-naked on the couch! You've got to get that kid out and I now have to deal with my wife!"

Carl was stunned, but perhaps not shocked. He got CPS to investigate and to get Wilbur out and into the temporary shelter – then, back in court.

After hearing the details of the case, the judge responded. "I am ordering CWS to make the placement for Wilbur in the Graham Youth Service Center Facility, a group home for youth with substance abuse issues as CWS has recommended."

Carl never heard about Mrs. Barton's job as the school principal, if she was arrested, or if the marriage survived. He was too busy dealing with other cases. He did, however, discover that Wilbur had succeeded in his placement, and through family counseling he was able to get back home with his mother.

Case closed!*


*This is based on a true story.*

# SHAME

## Brother Andrew

Andy as a child was not happy. His dad was mean and his mom was not protective. He tended to be gentle and mostly fearful in his life. He was bullied at school and had no special friendships. He liked being alone. It felt much safer than to join with others. He did have a kind heart deep inside, if he saw a younger child on the playground needing help with the slide or swings, Andy was there to help. That was the level of his interactions with people. Even as he progressed into high school, he was a loner and just interacted in a class setting where he felt safer than in other activities. Studying alone and making good grades were his main themes. His parents continued their uncomfortable behaviors and took little interest in Andy. They both were Catholics and attended regularly making Andy also attend.

After graduation, Andy escaped from his home, applied, and was accepted into the Honaker Catholic Monastery. Because of his regular Catholic Church attendance, forced by his parents, he was invited to join the monastery. Now he was Brother Andrew. He began helping in the financial department where he could stay away from much contact with anyone. He also applied and was accepted into the college education program and learned more about the financial aspects. When he could, he was able to isolate in his "cell" as he called it. So his life was learning, serving, and seclusion. He somewhat reluctantly attended religious services, finding his own prayerful and spiritual rituals in this seclusion best.

One aspect of his painful and isolated life was the struggle with his sexual urges. Yes, he masturbated just for relief, but in his youth, he found several girls strongly attractive and they became his masturbating fantasies. This part of his life shamed him, but somehow he was able to accept it as a part of being a human being. His answer was to keep it under control, just enough to relieve his urges. Sexuality is very tricky among those dedicated to abstinence, he knew this and prayed and prayed for comfort and forgiveness.

A challenge that emerged was Sister Katharine, a lovely nun about his age who worked as an office assistant. Even dressed in her nun's habit she was attractive. Brother Andrew was very taken by her looks and her pleasant personality, plus her work skills. He found himself immersed in her presence. He could tell she liked him, too – well only in a friendly way, he hoped. He even started calling her Kate and she called him Andy – but only when others were not around.

One time they ran into each other in the local village food court. He asked her if she wanted to have lunch together. She said yes with a broad smile. Oh, his heart jumped and he also felt the overwhelming need to control his sensual thoughts. They sat at a table side by side and then each went to select their meals and drinks. Then they sat and ate, with just a few comments about work and the weather. Having finished their food and sipping the last of their sodas he suddenly felt something unusual, her hand on his beneath the table. This was like a strike of lightening to him. Her hand reached his and she pulled him toward her thigh. Then she looked him straight in the eye: "This is what is happening, isn't it, "she said. He looked deeply into her eyes, his heart thumping, his mind whirling, "YES!' he whispered. "Let's talk," she said.

They spent the afternoon describing how each had become a nun and monk, the pains of childhood and youth, they had so much in common. "We must leave this role, and find a new life together," she said. And in a shaded corner, they kissed – the first kiss for both of them. The comfort of the hug and kiss drew them to the reality of what was real in their life – not religious seclusion and a life of lack of love and sensual pleasure.

Both Andy and Kate resigned and had to search for a way to work together. Kate had a savings account from funds provided by an aunt, who saw her sorrowful life and wanted to gift her – her aunt had no children so Kate was the only relative she found to pour out her love. Her aunt had died a couple of years ago and offered her estate to Kate. With this to go on, they got married and were able to find housing. Now they began to wonder how to proceed.

The answer came in a united vision between them. They formed an organization, True Self and Service (TSAS) dedicated to helping those caught up in painful situations. The theme was helping people read their emotions and change to find a true life to live. Some were those treated poorly as children. Others had found they were unable to make their way in life choices or had defected from religious sects. Soon the TSAS was established in several cities and the grants and donations poured in. This all happened because of one hand reaching out to another in honest seeking.

# My, How Time Flies!

Insects have a community for contests. The one all insects love to watch or compete in is the flying race. Bees, wasps, butterflies, moths, beetles, mosquitoes, flies, and dragonflies compete in an annual contest. Oh, the gathering; all flying insects choose who will be in the competition. They race within each insect type to determine who will compete, and then the races begin.

To start, the butterflies go against the beetles, the moths go against the wasps, the mosquitoes go against the flies, and the dragonflies go against the bees. In each case, they have a method for determining who will be the judge of each contest. So, for example, the moths would judge the butterflies and beetle race. It is very important for the judge to be accurate and good at using the insect clock device, a device that has been kept hidden in a tree hole between each contest so no human or animal could find and steal or destroy it. The clock device was invented by ants and then sold to the flying insects for lots of sweet treats. Now it is hidden by each finalist winner of the flying insect race.

So this season all the insects (those interested) gathered near Lake Siouan. The winners this season for the finals were beetles and dragonflies. A great celebration was organized and all interested parties showed up. Each insect type brought their favorite foods to share – even a favorite honey-based drink, brought by the bees that caused insect drunkenness. Insect lovers danced and made love beneath the leaves of bushes. All insects celebrated, even the losers because it was joyful to have such a diverse and friendly gathering. No biting, no stinging, just "buggily" fun as they called it.

Then the celebration came to an end to prepare for the final race, to determine this season's winner; just one beetle against one dragonfly. Each insect species had to choose their contestant based on how well they did in the contests and then the judge had to be selected, too. So, the results: Bucton the Beetle vs. Devon the Dragon Fly. And the judge this season, Fervanti the Fly!

Let me tell you something very unusual. The prize this season was a gathering of the most luscious, sweet treats. Both Bucton and Devon were excited to have this to share with their family. They were so excited; in fact Bucton's family secretly met with Fervanti and offered a good amount of the treat if she would make sure they were the winner. Fervanti was known for her beauty and not so much for her honesty and when they met with her, she was still kind of in a drunken stupor from the honey drink. She readily agreed to do her best to make that happen. Fervanti was, however, known for her abilities, quick and clever.

"*Let The Race Begin*," yelled the seasoned organizer, Muskette the Mosquito. Bucton and Devon flew to the starting line and Fervanti was stationed at the finish line with the clock device. The race was around ten large oak tree trunks. Watchmen ants were hired to watch to see that the racers cleared the tree trunks. All grew silent and then Muskette cried out, "*READY, SET......GO!*"

Off went Bucton and Devon, and there sat Fervanti with her insect clock device. The bugs screamed and yelled and many had placed bets, which increased the buggily intensity! And then the two contestants raced toward the finish line. Devon seemed the obvious winner, but Fervanti yelled, "the winner...Bucton the Beetle! The whole crowd was astonished and they all yelled: *"My, How Fly Times!!"*

# Rules

Marko Dratful was the minister of a well-attended church in a Midwest Town. It was called The Righteousness of God Church and Marko spoke with great charisma which drew folks in. His wife Tollie was a blessing to folks, kind, and a great listener with a good heart. The main message of Marko was rules, rules, and rules in order to get to heaven. Break the rules you're going to hell! He focused on the Old Testament and preached about the Ten Commandments, how to eat, the importance of men as head of the household, how to dress, and proper behavior during Sundays and on and on. The topics were designed to make folks do the right thing and your reward will be great in Heaven. Their two kids, boys aged ten and thirteen were also taught to model the right behavior. In other words, you must work to get a blessing, that's it.

    Then one evening Tollie was crying. The kids had gone to bed (at the proper time) and she and Marko were in the living room. "What's wrong," Marko asked. "Oh, dear I have something to tell you about a vision I had based on my reading of the Apostle Paul's writing. I was shocked and felt a spiritual force to tell you about it." "What," Marko asked. "Oh, dear in Galatians 3:10, Paul says, 'All who rely on observing the law are under a curse' and in Galatians 5:6 he says, 'The only thing that matters is faith expressing itself in love.' And further, in Gal 5:1, 'It is for freedom that Christ has set us free.' My dear, it is not rules but love that counts!"

Marko was at first ready to explode in anger but somehow he fell to his knees and said, "I must go to my prayer cabin and ponder what you've said. If this is so, all I've done is wrong, – so I must go now!" Off he went in the night to his little cabin by a lake, where he would have no interruptions. As he prayed and pondered, he realized from what Tollie discovered that one view is that we must work to get a blessing, but with Jesus, we obviously are blessed and so we respond with works of love.

He came back the next day. The kids were off at school and he confessed his wrong views and decided to meet with the elders' committee and wanted Tollie to join him. They called a meeting and Tollie described her discovery and Marko shared his shock and confession. The elders were amazed but somehow they completely accepted this new view and decided it must be shared with the church members.

At the next church gathering the new view was shared. Of the two hundred members about fifty left in disgust, but the remaining members cheered, hugged, and wept with joy, a new way to be! The church was renamed: The Blessing of God Church. A new message was shared and the church grew so much with the sharing of loving actions in the town and beyond, they knew they were blessed and got to loving work!

# School Library

Anderson, Indiana was a much-divided city. There were black and white neighborhoods – typical during the 1960s and 1970s. Carl Rumford worked as a social worker for the local family service agency that served both communities as needed. On a few occasions, the agency responded to a request from the white elementary school to hold a behavior guidance session with some of the rascal kids. Carol Thompson was their student counselor at the white elementary schools. She appreciated it when Carl was the one who responded. She saw him as a nice guy and competent in dealing with naughty kid groups.

Sometimes the sessions were held in the school library where there was a resource specialist/librarian and quite a great collection of books and materials for kids in a marvelously spacious room with shelves, desks, and displays. Carl liked that venue, because of its nice atmosphere, which seemed to calm the kids. He'd put them in a circle of chairs and begin his session with each kid sharing their cares and fears that caused them to misbehave and he guided them toward understanding. Carol would often join him and assist with the process and mainly work with the girls. They were both professionals doing their jobs, and there was a bit of attraction between the two, but no outward indications.

For the first time, the black school contacted the agency to get some help with troubled and misbehaving kids who had been disciplined. Carl was assigned that job. He was told by the vice principal that they'd meet in the library. When Carl arrived he was told by the office clerk that the kids were in the library already with the vice principal and he could go downstairs to meet with them. He went down the stairs and he was now in the school basement and the kids were in the furnace room. He entered and there was a bookcase with three shelves and about twenty or thirty books – that was it, that was their library! Carl was shocked, but he set up the circle of chairs for the kids and started the session. The vice principal just waited for directions to help. Afterward heading back to the agency he became angry at what he'd just experienced – institutional racism in the vilest way! The white elementary kids had scores of books and materials and a librarian, and the black kids had thirty books and no librarian – ugh!

Carl knew he had to do something, but what? He called Carol and asked her to meet with him after school and on his workday. They met in the coffee shop and he described what he had witnessed. She too was shocked and disgusted by it. Her white kids were offered rich resources and the black kids none! Carol said, "Carl, what can be done to correct this?"

"That's why I wanted to meet with you, Carol, to see if we could find an answer, together."

"Oh my, what a challenge, and I'm in the middle of it. Oh dear!"

Carl offered this, "Let me come up with a plan, and if I do, would you be willing to review it and then we could work together."

"Okay, Carl." That became the beginning of a partnership.

THE PLAN: Carl spent time researching social change

occurrences in various situations. He found educational change-making quite a challenge but he came up with a few ideas. He contacted Carol and said, "Our first step is to talk to the Superintendent and then secondly, go to the school board president and explain our concern."

Carol agreed but nervously said, "I hope I don't get fired for this."

"Oh my, me too, but we gotta do something."

"Yes, you are right, Carl; so set it up."

Carl made an appointment to meet with the superintendent (he went alone to protect Carol) and the superintendent thanked Carl for his report and then added, "It is what it is." In other words, he didn't give a crap about the library differences.

Next, Carl made an appointment with the president of the school board – basically, the same response, and the president even told him angrily, "Get off this issue, I may have to talk to your director, if you don't!" Carl was so angry and he called and told Carol about the responses. She was shocked and annoyed but, "Then what next?" "I'll get back to you, Carol after I've thought about it.

"Okay, let me know."

Carl decided after much thought and research – the only thing he saw as a possibility was to create a protest by concerned citizens, but how? He called Carol again and suggested they meet and discuss his idea. Carol was shaken but decided to take it step by step. Something had to be done.

After meeting they decided to connect with the PTA's white and black school groups. They first met with the black PTA leader, who didn't really realize how terrible it was and she said she would meet with her PTA members and see about a protest option. Next, they met with the white PTA and surprisingly the leader was also shocked and said she'd meet with her group. Both PTA meetings were called and Carl and Carol showed up to answer questions. Both groups were annoyed at the disparity and they agreed to protest at the next regular meeting of the school board.

Here's what happened: There were nearly one thousand protesters who showed up with signs that read: *Equality For Black Students*. The school board members were shocked and actually realized that the disparity had to be dealt with. The board members were maybe more fearful of their positions than the morality of it, but they decided to review the budget and make needed changes. A new library budget was approved for the black school and even a librarian was assigned. Carl and Carol were able to keep their heads down and let the citizens take credit.

After the changes were approved and made, Carl told Carol, we've got to celebrate and party over this. I'll pick you up Saturday night and we'll head for the Bakersfield Restaurant and Bar for fun! They ate, drank, and danced, and then Carol looked directly into Carl's eyes and said, "Carl, I love you!" Carl said, "I love you and want us to be together for good!"

"Agreed, you great guy!" And Carl responded, "Agreed you great girl!" And then the first kiss!

Carl and Carol had their wedding in the black school library!*

*Partially based on a true story.*

# Null

Professor Tony Rancor taught a weekly Sociology class in the local community college. He worked as a social worker full time and this was a way to fill a personal need but also was enjoyable for him. He had just started and was working his way through the planned curriculum for the first time. He came to the section on Social Science Research, the first few sessions were pretty simple and easy. Then the session on the Null Hypothesis came up.

Tony didn't spend much time on this one before the next class; he was also a busy social worker, family guy, and he just quickly covered each topic for the class. But this one caught him by surprise. The Null Hypothesis is a fairly complex concept (*look it up and you'll see why*). So in desperation, being right in the middle of the class session and confused he sort of faked it – reading off some of the concepts, and then he became completely befuddled. To survive and not get embarrassed he gave a handout paper to students after forming small groups. He told them to discuss the concept while he took a break. What he didn't tell them was that he didn't understand it at all.

Professor Rancor left the room and went to the men's restroom where he found himself sweating and thirsting from the anxiety of hiding his ignorance to save face. He coughed and scooped water into his mouth with his hands, breathing heavily in his shame and self-disgust. What should he do? His next step was to return to the class and say, "This class is dismissed and I'll see you next week to answer your questions and discuss the

Null Hypothesis." The students were naturally confused and left shaking their heads. They were not going to challenge a professor about what seemed an odd way to handle this class session. Rancor knew his passion had outweighed the students' need to get an explanation. His shame continued on his way back home, and he didn't even tell his wife and kids about the issue – but it weighed heavily on his conscious.

Sunday morning at church the last hymn at the end of the service was, <u>I Surrender All</u> with the phrase, "Lord, I give myself to Thee." Tony's heart broke, and the shame he felt for his dishonesty caused him to nearly run to the church altar railing where he knelt down and began sobbing. The service was ending and people were confused. A couple of Elders came up to Tony and put their hands on his shoulder as he sobbed. Inside Tony felt a great desire to silently confess his error and he decided to just "let go" of his egotism at that moment. He felt like *nothing* and it felt so good. He stood up and said just that to confused Elders, "I am nothing and it feels so good!" What he felt was a sense of emptying himself to God. He left the church with his family and he then told his wife about his mistake and his sense of emptying. His wife hugged him, "You are coming to terms with yourself, aren't you?" "Yes!" he answered.

Professor Rancor went back to class. He stood up and said, "Oh dear students, I want to confess and apologize for my ignorance about the Null Hypothesis and my inability to tell you so. I hereby tell you I don't understand the Null Hypothesis and I won't try to teach it to you. I am so sorry and I promise from now on I will be honest with you about my ignorance. Would you forgive me?"

The students looked shocked; a professor confessing had never happened to them. They stood up and rushed toward him hugging him and each saying "I forgive you."

"OK, let's start anew, students!" Tony said.

"*YES*!" They shouted.

A new day for their Sociology class began! A *professor confessor* opened the way!*

*\*Based on a true story.*

# Reward

Greta was a young and lovely college girl. She needed to work in order to help pay for college classes. So, her latest job was at the Brighten Senior Lodge, a very luxurious home for the elderly. Only the rich could afford it and basically, Caucasian elders were housed there. The staff, however, was mostly needy students, Latinos, and Black folks. Greta worked in the culinary department, mostly serving meals and cleaning up after the messy eaters. Two of her favorite staff members were black women (Carla and Colby), both of whom were very helpful in teaching Greta how to do the job in the best way.

Carla and Colby had worked at Brighten for several years and put in many hours each week. Greta was only parttime, usually for the dinner hour, serving, and cleaning. The residents were not so fond of the minority servants and basically accepted Greta, but most of them were very demanding of the staff: wanting meals served more quickly, having the tastiest tidbits, and wanting dirty dishes cleared as soon as possible. Carla and Colby taught Greta to put up with the nasty residents; it was a job "so just do it."

The time came for "rewards night" for staff. Annually. the residents would offer funding since tipping was not allowed, just this special gift. Envelopes with cash were passed out to each of the residents with thank you cards. Greta got $400 and when she met up with Carla and Colby they had each gotten $50. Greta was shocked and disgusted – they put in the long hours and many months of work and she only had been there for a few months — and parttime!

Greta immediately went to Mr. Brig's office, the Brighten staff supervisor, told him of the incident, and said, "The gifting was definitely an indication of institutional racism!"

Brigs barked back, "That is a terrible thing to say – you are not too bright, Greta!"

"Well, I quit!" Greta screamed back – "I'm out of here, you've seen the last of me!"

"Very well, we'll send your final paycheck to you – so be gone."

Greta took her envelope and met up with Carla and Colby. She took the 4 $100 bills and gave each of them $200. "You are so deserving of this, not me!" Greta said. Carla and Colby gratefully took the money, mostly because they knew the heart of Greta and wanted to show agreement for her judgment. All three hugged.*

*Based on a true story.

# TINY TRUE TALES

## Ten True Tales of Minor Wonders

### CHICO

As an older child, I had a wonderful dog named Chico. As a younger child, I lost a favorite pet named Buffy when he lay in the road outside our country home and was run over. Chico was a marvelous replacement. During those later times with Chico, we lived in a 28-foot trailer (trailer trash?) and had to move often as my dad's job changed. One night I was awakened by my mom – "Get up; the guys are here to move our trailer. I got up and searched for Chico. He had disappeared. I went out calling out for him: "Chico, Chico!" After I searched unsuccessfully my dad ordered me into the car: "Get in it's time to go now!" I nearly collapsed in sadness then felt Chico's paws on my knee! "Chico!"

### ESP

My mother was psychic, yes; the real thing. She could find lost objects, toys, and things my older sister and I might lose. Once she woke up and called the police telling them where to find a lost child. Once in my high school carnival booth, we used her to answer kids' questions at 25 cents per question — one girl asked her what she was getting for her birthday. My mom told her of a trip to California. The girl's mom came angrily back screaming, "You gave away our birthday secret!" I asked what I would do when I was grown up. She said I'd write a book. Wow, I've written several books and many were published!

## LETTERMAN

Back in the day, a high school could include freshman 9$^{th}$ graders. I started my high school in the 9$^{th}$ grade and graduated after 4 years, the *wonder*? I lettered each year as a first-string football line guard, a four-year letterman!

## PUBLIC SPEAKING

I was a shy kid when it came to speaking before people and it continued into my early adult years. For example, as a 7–year-old , I remember being asked to read a scripture in a line of kids taking turns at church. I walked up to the podium, looked at the congregation, and immediately walked back down — a shame for my parents. As a college student, I was hired by the YMCA to work with youth groups. In a staff gathering, I was asked to read the 23$^{rd}$ Psalm as a devotional. I sputtered and barely managed to make it through. My boss, a caring guy instructed me to speak as much as possible. I obeyed and whenever there was an opportunity I suffered through it, but I got so comfortable that I became a trainer and speaker throughout my life, facing hundreds of people in audiences.

## LOVE AND MARRIAGE

When I was in high school I had a love and lost that love, leaving me fearful of any relationship with girls. My YMCA boss (mentioned in the story above) counseled me with some strength. I needed to have a set of criteria for a woman I would want to connect romantically with. So, I made up those criteria including spiritual qualities, personal qualities, and several other qualities. So, I braved up and dated girls. I would ask my "quality" questions and was good at listening.

No one met my criteria until the next one. I was volunteering at the Seattle World Expo in 1962 at the Christian Witness Pavilion venue. I was the guy who said "goodbye and blessings" as folks left. A young lady at the souvenir shop invited me to her Sunday school class the next Sunday. I arrived but she wasn't there. There was a cute girl I noticed who smiled nicely at me. I met her outside the class afterward and asked her out for a coffee. (Ironically, she had a boyfriend, who also didn't show up that Sunday.) Well, as I dated her and asked her my quality questions, she answered everyone correctly. I then decided she was the one I wanted to marry. She refused to say yes; she had other plans, for traveling to Brazil (she had studied Brazilian Portuguese language) – more important than me. But she took a trip with a friend and on that trip, her friend told her that she shouldn't miss the opportunity to be married to someone like me (a special guy!). When we met next — she simply said, "Jim, I want to marry you." I leapt and shouted and danced around the room! We got married!

Another thing that happened, years into our marriage, I went to a fundraiser gathering and they sold tickets to a drawing. I bought a couple of twentydollars$ tickets. My name was called and I won an eight hundred dollar sapphire necklace. The sapphire gem is my wife's birthstone! (After a wonderful life of fifty seven years together I lost her to cancer - but even in my grief I am grateful for those wonderful years of marriage and family wonders).

## CAREER

As I started my social work career, I floated toward teaching and training in that field— it just seemed to fit me. I also taught social work in an Oregon four-year college and after the college collapsed I was hired as a trainer in the state social services organization. After a few months, they decided to send trainers out to the various areas in the state. When I first met with the regional staff managers, one person complained that having a trainer was a waste of money. "Our area could use the money we're wasting on a regional trainer." Wow, I had to create a training program that would overcome that complaint. So I got busy developing helpful programs for all levels of staff. It worked! And from there I developed also a train-the-trainer model and wrote a book (Teach with Style) that got published two times based on a theory that I invented in my backyard. You'll find a bit of that model in the Yppy story, in here.

## TRAVEL

I never considered traveling the world my thing but it was my wife's dream. She began by living in Mexico and attending the

University of Mexico as a Spanish Language exchange student. We did live a couple of years in Hawaii getting my social work degree after we married. Then having and raising kids made it hard to go traveling. But after our four kids were between ages 5 and 12; Rebecca announced she'd like to spend a month in Portugal. She also had learned the Portuguese language. I said, "That's impossible, we haven't got the money!" She, having learned to play the guitar, put an ad in the local newspaper for folks who wanted to learn to play guitar. In just a year she had enough money for both of us to go to Portugal for a month! We took the kids to her parents' farm. They had agreed to watch them while we were gone.

From then on, at her motivation, we traveled to 30 countries and 5 continents! One quick tale – On our last trip before she died, we were returning from Wales at Heathrow Airport. We needed a ride to our car when we reached Seattle. In walked her cousin, from her Hungary visit, we boarded the same plane and she took us to our car!

## CHINA

We were sitting in church when the pastor announced that the Friends Church Yearly Conference needed English teachers at Wuhan University in Wuhan, China. We looked at each other and said yes to ourselves — offered to go— it was a school year assignment. First, we had a home and secondly, we had jobs. Here's what happened: A woman organist and her friend needed a home near her church for the exact time we needed to be gone; secondly we both got leaves of absence with a promise to return to our jobs at the end of our stay. Off we went, to what I call the "best year of my life!" We were adored by our students, because we taught them in a fun and humorous way, so different from their Chinese traditional teachers.

## POETRY

I used poetry in my China teaching. It just seemed like a good way to introduce the English language. The China students loved it and their Asian minds seemed just right for it. I used Haiku also. One girl with her English name, Dora was named Dora Duck after this great Haiku she offered:

> *I raised up a duck*
> *I want it to be my friend*
> *Why you cook it?*

For some reason, I'd never been a poet myself, but when I came back from China I wrote my first poetry chapbook, "Doing, Being, Loving." I went on to publish several other chapbooks and my last poetry offering published was based on the Tao Te Ching writings of the Chinese author Lao Tzu, I called it, "Because of This: How to Live, Love, and Lead." One of my Chinese students had introduced me to Lao Tzu's work. My poetry; born in China!

## LINE

One time I was suffering from chest pains and coughing. I went to the doctor and after an X-ray, it showed that I had a line in my lung and needed to go to a specialist. In the meantime, I was attending a church annual gathering and my pastor's wife, Charlene asked me how I was doing. I told her about the line in my lungs. She immediately told me to kneel and she prayed for my healing right then. I showed up at the pulmonologist's office and he did another X-ray, no line in my lung! Healed!

*Note: After reading these stories, think about your own moments of Wonder!*

# Ten True Tales of Minor Danger

### RIVER ICE

When I was a young child we lived in the country and behind our home was a river. I loved hanging out in the woods and playing by the river. One day in the winter the river was covered with ice. What a fun thing to walk on river ice. I stepped out on it and began my little trek— then the shrill call of my mother, "Jimmy get off the river, now!" I did what she demanded and lived.

### ROCK THROW

When I was an older child perhaps about 9 or 10 years old, we lived in a trailer park above a highway. I was kind of a loner with not many kids in that trailer park. Just to pass the time I went to the edge of the cliff above the highway and threw rocks down just for fun. Then the last rock I threw hit and broke the side mirror of a car passing by. I was stunned and ran back toward our trailer. The car came up into the trailer park and the guy saw me and drove up and asked, "Did you throw that rock?" I answered, "No sir, it might have been another kid, not me." He drove away.

## AUTO CRASH

When I was a teenager, old enough to drive I was driving my mom and my girlfriend somewhere. In those days, we all three sat in the front— driver seat and passenger bench seat. I zipped along and came to an intersection with no red light, assumed it was go-green. I entered the intersection and was slammed by a pickup truck on my back fender, spinning us around. Two spare ties flew out of the trunk and the bench seat collapsed back with my mom and girlfriend – none hurt. Determined: the traffic light was out and the city was at fault.

## SWIM OH!

This was during my college days and I majored, at first, in physical education. During a pool time swim, I had completed several laps and was worn to a frazzle and as I headed back toward the edge a fellow student, just for fun, jumped on me grabbing my shoulders; I was already out of breath (breathing heavily) and he was pulling me down. If I went under, I would have breathed in water. With all my remaining strength I managed to just barely grab the side of the pool – Alive!

## GYMNASTICS

Two incidents caused me to discontinue on the college gymnastics team: First: I was doing my tricks on the parallel bars and did a kip (a special two-leg flip that causes you to fly above the bars so you can grab and continue the routine – well, my hands missed the bars and I came flying down; fortunately I landed perfectly flat on my back on the mat below. My two buddies nearly fell over laughing. Second: I was really good at back handsprings to a full back somersault — that's what I did: flip, flip, flip to my somersault and landed on my head – OW! That was my last effort at gymnastics.

## SURFER

Our first two years of marriage were spent in Hawaii, where I was in graduate school. We loved swimming and body surfing. I'd never tried regular surfing with a surfboard but when we were vacationing on Maui, I decided to rent a surfboard and give it a try. I'd seen lots of surfers do it and it looked simple— paddle out with the board, wait for a wave, and climb aboard for the ride. Well, that's what I did a large wave came and I rode it until I slipped off and the board disappeared into the deep. But the surfboard reappeared rising up at a breakneck speed – just missing my head – had it hit me, I'd be dead. No more surfing!

## SNOW, OH!

Heading back from Chicago to home in Anderson, Indiana, got caught in a heavy snowstorm. It was so heavy that the windshield wipers on my VW Bug, couldn't keep it off. So, to help me see my way through, I needed to do something or just stop. I chose the manly way and banged on the windshield from inside to knock off the heaping snow; and broke the windshield. Somehow I got home.

## SMOKE-FREE MEDITATION

I was a heavy smoker. Back in the day you could smoke anywhere and I did; in the house, in the car with kids, in restaurants – anywhere. But I was getting tired of being a smoker – I had a sense of guilt and my darling wife endured but I knew she knew it wasn't a good thing. So, I decided to throw all my cigarettes away, go to Silver Falls Park, and meditate under a waterfall. Several of the falls had protected areas where you could sit behind a waterfall. I went to one and began to quiet my mind and breathe. Then I was attacked by mosquitos, so intense, I had to run away. I got in my car and stopped at the first gas station store, bought a pack of Marlboros and got to smoking again. Finish: I took a seven-day Adventist Church class on stopping smoking – saw photos of the lungs of smokers – all black – I lastedthree 3 days and stopped smoking forever!

## POT

I was a drinker and a pot smoker during my Oregon State working days. When I'd smoke pot someone offered (I never bought it) I would get such intense hunger for sweets. One session away from home I indulged in both drink and pot. I had a strong craving for chocolate cream pie offered at a nearby bakery. I was driving the boss's State Car and headed out in the night fog for my pie! I began to feel faint and was overwhelmed by deep fog and came to a slowing, slowing, stop, right in the middle of the highway. But somehow I came back to consciousness…and managed to get to the bakery and my pie! I could have lost my job and my career if someone had reported me, or hit me on the foggy night. End of the smoking pot!

## COURT CASE

When I was a State Childcare Licensor, I was handed a case transferred from another office – perhaps a move of the person's home child care into my area. I reviewed the case and found suspicion of child molestation in both the owner and her husband. Why had that office allowed them to remain licensed? I decided to order a sexual deviancy evaluation. They refused, so I suspended the license based on the suspected dangers. We went to the local court and I won, but they appealed and we ended up in the State Supreme Court, where I won again. The husband came to me and said, "We will prevail, Mr. Teeters!" My attorney warned me to let them leave. We stood above the entry safety check entrance and watched the husband collect a big knife he'd checked there. Glad I didn't go down.

*Note: After reading these stories, think about your own minor dangers you faced and survived.*

# Ten True Tales of Minor Shame

### BACK OF THE BUS

When I was about fifteen years old my mother and I boarded a Greyhound Bus to visit my sister who'd gotten married and moved to the Midwest where her husband was in school to become a chiropractor. There were only four people on the bus, my mom and I, and two young women. One woman had on a dress that was very low on her breasts – I could see her sexy image in the bus mirror. I wandered to a back seat and, well I masturbated gazing at her image.

One other thing – when we got to my sister's her husband wanted me to be one of his patients for practice. He torqued my neck so hard that I actually got sick and threw up. I never, ever went to a chiropractor again. Might have been my moral punishment?

### BREAK SIGN

I was walking with a couple of friends during my teenage years. We came upon a for sale sign poked into the ground. Just because I was a tough guy, I wanted to show off my strength, so I pulled out the sign and started smashing it to pieces on the ground. As I smashed and my friends watched we heard a man cry out, "He feller, what you doin'!" It was obviously the owner of the sign.

Well, we just kept on walking, and no consequences. The guy might have been intimidated by these tough teenagers.

## ACADEMIC CHEAT

When I was in graduate school at the University of Hawaii, we were given a test. I was perplexed by a particular question that was an important one to answer right. I was sitting next to one of the smartest Asian girls. She was working on the answer to that question and, yes I secretly looked at her paper while she was busy writing and entered the answer she gave and I passed the test wondrously, er... shamefully!

## BAD DAD I – SON, MORGAN

I was playing with my youngest son, Morgan. He had model figures based on characters from a story of futuristic wonderment. I was using a magical character that could do spectacular things. My son was using the lead character in our play story. We were playing as oppositional characters and I took my magical guy who pointed at Morgan and said, "You shall remain stupid!" Morgan only five or six at the time was dumbfounded and didn't know what to say.

## BAD DAD II A POEM – SON, MARLAN

**Sackcloth and Ashes**
None of us tear our garments anymore
when our sins weigh us down
or we are sick with sorrow
like those bible kings of old

They'd rip their clothes
pour ashes on their sorry heads
to let their shame or sadness show

That time I shook my teenage son too hard
when he refused to mow the lawn
might've called for that

It would've done me and him some good
if I'd ripped my tee shirt and jeans
dumped some fireplace
ashes in my hair;
then gone and knocked on his bedroom door
and said I'd been wrong

We could've laughed together
but instead, I lay awake
thinking about my misplaced rage
and I waited until he'd grown
into a man to humbly ask
him to forgive me

## AH…ER…#1

Our family of four kids went on a trip to my wife's family farm. On the way, we stopped to visit one of my fellow staff trainers and his wife. We had a nice visit and they fed us lunch, then we climbed back in our VW bus and headed for the farm.

I asked my wife for the map we needed and she noticed we'd left the map back at the couple's house (back then in the 1970s paper maps were used; no such thing as a GPS) and we needed it to navigate our way to the farm. So we turned around and when we entered the driveway the wife came running out, "Guess what you forgot?" "Our map," I said. Then out of their doorway came our youngest daughter who we'd left but didn't notice!

## INSULT TO GOD?

During my pastor years, I was a volunteer chaplain at a local hospital. My assignment was the oncology unit, quite a challenge. I listened to the patients and prayed for them. I remember one sweet lady with serious lung cancer from smoking. She told me with tears in both our eyes, "I really enjoyed my cigarettes, but now I don't."

Later one of the nurses asked me to visit a woman who was refusing to accept the syringe with the chemotherapy she needed. I went to her room where her husband was also visiting. I said I was the hospital chaplain and I've come to pray with you. She looked shocked and pulled the covers up to her chin and blurted out, "Are you born again?" "Yes," I answered and she dropped the covers and smiled. We chatted a bit and I prayed for her recovery. I went back to the nurses' station and told her nurse this: "If you want her to take those meds, just tell her the syringe is *born again*."

## INSULT TO FRANCE?

My wife and I traveled to Paris and I had always enjoyed the art of Marcel Duchamp. He had some very interesting 3-D objects even a urinal as part of his collection. His works were located in the Museum of Modern Art and we went there to check it out. I wasn't clear on where Duchamp's collection was located, so I found a museum staff member and asked, "Where can I find Marcel Duchamp's display?"

He glanced at me but turned away slightly. My wife, who was standing nearby came over and said to the guy, "*Bonjour, Masseur*; where can we find Marcel Duchamp's display?" He immediately directed us to Duchamp.

## LIAR, LIAR

I worked with displaced kids and other family issues of those in need. I had one six-year-old kid, Tommy (not his real name) who had been adopted and then rejected by his adoptive family. He was placed in foster care. Several times when I came to work on Monday morning I was told Tommy had been placed in a different foster home – it had something to do with his behavior. To get a special in-home therapist (quite expensive for the agency) he needed to be diagnosed with a particular behavior issue. I created a document, stating that he had that particular behavioral issue (a lie) and submitted it. He was awarded the in-home therapist to serve Tommy and the foster parents – he remained stable! Just a note: I was also able to find him a new and successful adoptive family! It took a lie!

### AH...ER...#2

I spent several years as a family child daycare licensor for the state agency. Every three years, a provider had to have a review of their licensing qualifications. They needed to meet all of the state requirements: this included all family members having a current background check for any criminal or risky issues. I arrived at Martha's (not her real name) home child care and began going through the checklist. I asked her why her husband's background check was not on file. She said nothing but turned toward her desk and seemed to be sniffling. She reached for a Kleenex and I thought perhaps she was having allergy problems. I asked her again, "Martha, where is your husband's background check?" She turned around and sobbed, "My husband died last year and it's in the file." Oh, my...I looked and sure enough, I had missed the notation of her husband's death as I carelessly perused her file. I almost fell on my knees begging her to forgive me, and she did!

*Note: After reading these stories think about your moments of shameful behavior.*